The Sleeping Beauty

Retold by Freya Littledale

Pictures by Brenda Dabaghian

SCHOLASTIC INC.

New York Toronto London Auckland Sydney

ISBN 0-590-32949-9

Text copyright © 1984 by Freya Littledale. Illustrations copyright © 1984 by Scholastic Inc. All rights reserved. Published by Scholastic Inc.

12 11 10 9 8 7 6 5 4 3   6 7 8/8

Printed in the U.S.A.   24

For my mother, Dorothy

F.L.

To my parents

B.D.

A king and a queen once wished for a child.
But for a long time their wish did not come true.

Then one morning,
as the queen was bathing in the garden pool,
a frog jumped out and spoke to her.
"Oh, Queen, you will get your wish," the frog said.
"By the time the wild roses are in bloom
you shall have a child."

And that is just what happened.
When the wild roses were in bloom
the queen had a baby girl.

The queen named the baby Briar Rose.
"We must have a great feast," the king said.
"I want all our friends to come
and see the new princess."

"Yes, yes," the queen said.
"And we must invite the wise fairies too.
They like to bring magic gifts
to newborn children."

Now there were thirteen fairies in the kingdom,
but the king's messengers invited only twelve.
They could not find the oldest fairy.
"She must have died," they told the king.
"No one has seen her in fifty years."

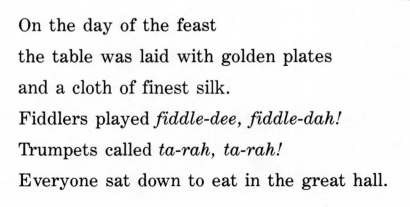

On the day of the feast
the table was laid with golden plates
and a cloth of finest silk.
Fiddlers played *fiddle-dee, fiddle-dah!*
Trumpets called *ta-rah, ta-rah!*
Everyone sat down to eat in the great hall.

When the feast was over
each fairy gave the princess a gift — a magic wish.
The first fairy wished her wisdom.
The second fairy wished her kindness.
The third fairy wished her beauty.
One by one, each of the fairies made her magic wish.
Just as the last fairy was about to speak,
the door flew open.
There stood the thirteenth fairy!
"How dare you invite everyone but me!" she cried.
She pounded her crooked cane on the marble floor.
"I am the oldest and most powerful of all!
Well I, too, have a gift for your child.

"At the age of fifteen," she said,
"the princess will prick her finger with a spindle —
and fall down dead."
With these words, the fairy turned and left.

Then the twelfth fairy stepped forward.

She had not yet given her gift.

"I would undo this evil spell if I could," she said.

"But my power is not great enough.

I can only make the spell less terrible."

The fairy then made her wish.

"When the princess pricks her finger, she will *not* die.

Instead, she will fall asleep

and sleep for one hundred years."

"Sleep for a hundred years!" the king said.

"I cannot let this happen!"

And he sent his horsemen out with these orders:

FIND EVERY SPINDLE AND SPINNING WHEEL

IN THE WHOLE KINGDOM —

AND BURN THEM ALL!

So the spindles were burned.

And the king was sure he had saved his daughter.

As the years passed
the fairies' wishes came true.
The princess was so beautiful, kind, and clever
that everyone loved her.
Even the cook loved her,
and the cook was not easy to please.

One day when Briar Rose was fifteen,
she was walking alone through the castle.
She came upon some dark stairs going up
to an old, dark tower.
The princess had never been in the tower.
But suddenly she wanted very much to see it.

She climbed the winding staircase up, up into the tower.
At the top she saw a little door.
A rusty key was in the lock.
The princess turned the key and the door opened wide.

She stepped inside a tiny room
filled with cobwebs.
An old, old woman sat at a spinning wheel,
spinning as fast as she could.

"Good day," said Briar Rose.
"What are you doing?"

The old woman nodded her head and smiled.
"I am spinning, my dear," she said.

"Oh, please, may I try?"
"I have never seen that before," said Briar Rose.

"Yes, indeed!" said the old woman.
"Come close and I will teach you."

The instant Briar Rose
reached out
she pricked her finger
on the sharp spindle.

Then she fell on the bed
and lay in a deep sleep.
The old woman disappeared.
And sleep spread over the entire castle.

The king and queen fell asleep on their thrones.
All the lords and ladies of the court fell asleep.

The doves on the roof,

the dogs in the kennel,

the horses in the stable —

they all fell asleep.

Even the flies on the wall fell asleep.

In the kitchen,

the fire stopped crackling.

And the roast beef stopped turning on the spit.

The kitchen boy, who had spilled some milk, fell asleep.

And so did the cook, who was about to pinch him

for being so clumsy.

Everything was silent.

All around the castle
a wall of briars began to grow.
Every year it grew higher and higher
till only the castle tower could be seen
from far away.

Meanwhile, the story of Briar Rose
spread near and far.
One prince after another tried to reach her.
But the thorns gripped them like sharp claws.
None of them could pass through the wall of briars.

After many, many years, a prince from a faraway land
came riding through the forest.
He saw the castle tower
behind the briar wall.
"What is that?" he asked.

"It is a haunted castle," said one of his men.

"It is a witch's castle," said another.

But the third, who was a very old man, said,
"It is an enchanted castle."

Then he told the story
he had heard as a child.
It was the story of the Princess Briar Rose.

"I must go and try to wake her," said the prince.

"Do not go!" said the old man.
"You will be trapped by the thorns
just like the others."

"I am not afraid," said the prince.
And on he went.

Now, the hundred years were almost over,
and the princess was soon to wake from her long sleep.
So when the prince came to the wall,
the thorns did not catch him.
The wall of briars opened to let him pass,
and wild roses bloomed on every branch.
Then the wall of roses closed behind him.

In the courtyard,
everything was so quiet
the prince could hear the beating of his heart.
But he kept on walking.

Inside the castle, the prince saw the king and queen
and their whole court sleeping.
The cook and the kitchen boy were sleeping.
And the kitchen maid was sleeping
with her hand filled with feathers
and a black hen in her lap.

There wasn't a single sound.

The prince walked through the castle
until he came to the winding staircase.
Up he climbed to the top of the old, dark tower.
He opened the door to the little room.
There lay Briar Rose.
The prince had never seen anyone as beautiful as she.
He leaned over and kissed her lips.

At once Briar Rose opened her eyes.
"Am I dreaming?" she whispered.

"No, my princess.
You are awake at last," said the prince.

The spell was broken!
The castle came to life again.
Dogs barked.
Horses neighed.
Doves cooed.
Flies buzzed.
The cook pinched the kitchen boy's arm,
and he yelled, "Ouch!"
The kitchen maid went on plucking the hen
while the fire rose up and cooked the meat.

The king and queen yawned and stretched.
"I feel as if I've slept
for a hundred years," said the king.

"So do I," said the queen. "I wonder . . ."
Quickly, they both got up from their thrones.
"Briar Rose! Briar Rose!" they called.

At that very moment
the princess stepped into the hall
with the prince at her side.

He told everyone what had happened.

"Amazing!" said the king.

"Now we must have a great feast." And they did.

The fiddlers played *fiddle-dee, fiddle-dah!*

The trumpets called *ta-rah, ta-rah!*

Briar Rose and the prince were married and . . .

they lived happily ever after.